# I Can Talk to God... anytime anyplace

by Jennie Davis
illustrated by
Carole Boerke

Published by The Dandelion House
A Division of The Child's World

for distribution by VICTOR BOOKS™
A Division of Scripture Press Publications Inc.

Distributed by Scripture Press Publications, Wheaton, Illinois 60187.

**Library of Congress Cataloging in Publication Data**

Davis, Jennie.
  I can talk to God—anytime, anyplace.

  Summary: A small boy enjoys the knowledge that God
is always there to listen to him, no matter what he has
to say.
  1. Prayer—Juvenile literature.  [1. Prayer.  2. God]
I. Boerke, Carole, ill.  II. Title.
BV212.M66            248.3'2            82-7245
ISBN 0-89693-205-2                      AACR2

Published by The Dandelion House, A Division of The Child's World, Inc.
© 1982 SP Publications, Inc. All rights reserved. Printed in U.S.A.

3 4 5 6 7 8 9 10 11 12 R 89 88 87 86

# I Can
## Talk
## to God··· anytime
### anyplace

I can talk to God. . .

anytime, anyplace.

I talk to God
in the morning. . .
when His world
wakes up!

I say, "Good morning, Lord.
Thank You for the sunshine.
Thank You for the birds."

Sometimes I thank God
for warm socks—
when the floor is cold!

That's how I talk to the Lord
when I get dressed.

God made all things—
even my food.
I thank Him
for my breakfast.

And then I thank Mom
for cooking it.

I can talk to God. . .

anytime, anyplace.

On the playground,
I thank Him
for the monkeybars
I love to climb. . .
and for the sand
that I make into
houses, castles,
and mountains.

I thank Him
for my friends
lots of times
when I play.

And I ask Him
to help me share with them.

When I go walking
with my Granddad,
we talk to God
together!
We thank Him
for parks to walk in. . .
for toadstools. . .
     and leaves
     and rocks
     and feathers.

And when we stop
for ice cream,
we thank God then, too!

Sometimes I talk to God
about His world. And I
help Him take care of it.

That's what I do when
I help Dad rake leaves.

I can talk to God. . .

anytime, anyplace.

When I'm very happy,
I sometimes
sing a song to God.
I like to talk
to Him by singing.

When I take a bath
and the water sloshes out,
I say, "Thank You, God,
for water. You made all
the water in the world."

And Mom says,
"Don't waste it!"

I can talk to God. . .
anytime, anyplace.

I can talk to God
even when I've done
something wrong.
He forgives me
and helps me say,
"I'm sorry."

It's nice
to know
God hears
my prayers—

for sick friends. . .

about hurt feelings. . .

and about lots of other things.

I talk to God
     because He listens. . .
         anytime, anyplace.

"The Lord will hear when I call to Him"
(Psalm 4:3).